# CHRISTMAS TRUCE
## A Novella in the Trench Raiders Series
### by Sean McLachlan

*For Almudena, my wife*
*And Julián, my son*

*24 December 1914*

Sergeant Hugh Willoughby trudged down a muddy communication trench, his breath coming out in frosty gusts as he labored to carry eighty pounds of weapons and gear.

The trenches were deeper than when he had seen them last. More extensive too. The quartermaster who had given him directions to the section of firing line held by the Oxfordshire and Buckinghamshire Light Infantry had told him there was still a good half mile to go.

Back when he had last been here two months ago, all the British Expeditionary Force had to defend was a muddy ditch they called a firing line, a half dozen miserable communication trenches so shallow you had to crawl most of the time, and a few craters sporting embryonic ditches they called a support trench.

But look at it now. His boots clomped along duckboard that kept him out of the worst of the mud, and every few yards another trench branched off to the left or right. A telephone wire snaked along one wall. Street signs were posted on intersections, advertising the way to Long Lane or Fleet Street or Piccadilly Circus. English names for a patch of Flanders nightmare.

There were more men too. When they'd been defending Ypres in October they'd only had the battered remnant of a few divisions. Half the time they didn't get their rations because there weren't enough men to fetch them. Messengers would disappear and not be replaced. Guns fell silent for lack of shells.

Now men swarmed along the warren of trenches. He kept to the side, brushing against the black strip of telephone wire as a work crew huffed along to some spot on the line, coming by twos with each pair of Tommies carrying a spool of barbed wire between them. Trudging the other way came a worn-out platoon headed to the rear for a well-earned rest.

A twinge in his side told him he could use some rest himself. The bullet that had got him in October, the one now encased in glass and taking pride of place on his parents' mantelpiece in Oxford, still felt like it was lodged in his belly. Every now and then some odd movement would remind him that he had been perforated and almost killed but for a good friend who had dragged him under fire back to a dressing station.

The way things had been shaping up in this war, he'd be dragging Crawford back to a dressing station before long. Oh wait, he'd already done that. So whose turn was it now then?

Bloody hell, but this pack felt heavy. Two months in hospital had sapped his strength. Lugging his Lee-Enfield, sixty pounds of regulation gear, as well as presents and other trifles from home, was proving to be exhausting. By the time he made it to the firing line he'd need another recovery period in Blighty.

A rat scurried across his path and he gave it an absentminded kick. Its squeal seemed to alert its comrades, because several more swarmed out from beneath some discarded sacking, scrabbled up the trench wall, over a line of tattered sandbags, and out of sight. The whiff of rotting flesh told him what they were after, and a sign told him why that mess that had once been a man hadn't been given a Christian burial. Crudely daubed in red paint on the side of an ammunition crate and nailed to a support bar on the trench wall were the words,

"This section exposed to snipers. Heads down."

Willoughby hunched his shoulders a little more. Good posture was only for the parade ground. While this trench was deeper than he was tall, he'd seen more than one man get his brains blown out passing an eroded section or a spot where the sandbags had fallen in.

"Merry Christmas, you bloody idiot," Willoughby muttered to himself.

He could be in Oxford right now. The doctor had asked him, *asked* him, mind you, whether he felt fit to return to duty. In the strange language of His Majesty's Army, a language as nuanced as French yet as precise as German, that question translated to, "Given your good breeding, the upcoming holidays, and your natural-born unfitness for this sort of work, if you want another month of sick leave I'll grant it to you."

Willoughby had said he was fit for service. His book was stamped, files were submitted, and three days later he found himself on a ship bound for Calais.

Why had he done such a fool thing? From a Christmas feast, a warm hearth, and gifts to. . .this.

"Willoughby!"

He turned, saw the subaltern's stripes, and saluted. Then he recognized the face beneath the service cap.

"Ellis!"

Willoughby lumbered over to the entrance of a dugout where his university friend stood and took his hand.

"I never thought I'd get a salute from you, Willoughby, not after the thrashings you gave me in the Debate Club!"

"It's good to see you, Ellis. How's things?"

"All right, considering. Applied for leave and didn't get it, which is no surprise. But how are you? It looks like you got better a bit too early."

Willoughby let out an embarrassed laugh.

"Where are you off to? Still in Thompson's outfit?" Ellis asked.

"Yes, going back."

"You chaps are making quite a name for yourselves. But do come in. We're having a bit of Christmas Eve tipple. Thompson can wait for a bit. There's a fine group of fellows here."

Ellis ushered him through the low, timber-framed doorway and down a short flight of steps made of cracked bricks. The interior of the dugout was a single room about ten feet to a side, framed with wood and lined with chicken wire. Niches were cut in the walls for sleeping quarters. Taking up the center was a table made of a door scavenged from some nearby house with sections of tree stump for legs. Around it sat five officers sharing a few bottles of wine and engaging in boisterous conversation.

Willoughby gave an automatic salute while he gaped at the officers' quarters. He'd heard living conditions had improved. The *Illustrated London News* had published photos of dugouts like this one, but he had thought they were just propaganda. Two months ago a "dugout" meant a little hole just big enough to squeeze into. This was the size of a middle-class sitting room.

Ellis' laughter rang out behind him.

"More salutes! I'll never get enough of them."

"Well, why shouldn't he bloody well salute?" a dour-faced captain said as he hunched over his wine glass.

"Oh, but you don't know him. He was with me at Magdalen College."

"Why, you're right, it's Willoughby!" a subaltern sitting next to the captain said.

"Hello, Chambers," Willoughby said, then nodded to another subaltern sitting opposite him. "Hello, Drake."

His two university friends rose up and shook his hand. Ellis introduced him to the other three men—two sergeant-majors named Billings and Anderson, and the grim captain, whose name was Dunning.

Two NCOs fussed in the background, preparing supper over a pair of spirit stoves. They were not introduced.

Ellis grabbed a crate and moved it over to the table so Willoughby could sit. He gratefully eased off his pack, tried not to wince at another twinge in his side, and tucked the pack and his rifle in a corner.

"Good to see you, old man," Ellis said as he sat down. "Have a drink."

An NCO fetched a tin cup and filled it with wine from one of the bottles on the table. Willoughby extended a hand to him.

"I'm Hugh Willoughby."

The man was a sergeant. He looked at Willoughby's sergeant stripes and gave a sidelong glance at Ellis. His face was a mask of uncertainty.

Taking his hand, he said, "Sergeant Maddox, sir."

Willoughby blushed. They were of the same rank but the man's working class accent and Willoughby's Oxonian one necessitated the "sir." He'd overcome that sort of nonsense with the men in his own platoon, but not anywhere else.

There was an awkward silence at the table. Captain Dunning filled it.

"I say, Ellis, is your friend a socialist?"

Sergeant Maddox slunk away.

"Of course not, but you know how Thompson's men are."

Dunning turned to him. "Yes, a bit lax on the discipline. Oxford lad, eh? I rowed for Cambridge in '03."

"Yes, you chaps made a fine win," Willoughby said, "that year."

Dunning gave him an evil look as Willoughby's fellow Oxonians tittered. Willoughby felt better now. The Boat Race was fair game and the closest thing to insubordination he would dare.

Dunning took another slug of his wine and studied him. "With your breeding, might I ask why you are only a sergeant?"

Willoughby felt his will harden.

"I enlisted as a private."

"Whatever for?"

Willoughby paused. What he'd like to say, what he really would say to a man of equal rank, was that he wanted to earn his commission, not get it just because of his background like these men. He knew Ellis and his other two friends were good officers, and no doubt the others, even Dunning, did their duty too, but he wanted to prove that he was good before the fact, not make up for it once he wore a subaltern's stripes.

But he couldn't say that. Not with three friends and a captain at the table. Instead he said, "If you have a rifle in your hand you get a chance to kill more Germans."

It came out sounding forced, which it was. He'd never been good at bravado. He took a gulp of wine to hide his embarrassment.

"An Oxbridge man such as yourself should be in a position of command," Dunning stated, tapping his finger on the table to emphasize his point.

"Yes, sir."

"He certainly comes from a family of commanders," Chambers laughed. "From what I hear his father runs his shops like a general and keeps all the workers at attention."

An even more awkward silence followed that. Willoughby had just been reminded that he was the only one at the table with a father who worked for a living. That had been happening all his life, no matter how good of an education Father bought him.

Ellis was quick to cover it up.

"The way Willoughby fights he'll outrank us all before long. Did you hear how he took two Maxims in as many days at the Aisne?"

Dunning raised an eyebrow. "Did he now?"

Ellis launched into the tale of Willoughby's first two trench raids, embellishing here and there for effect but getting the gist of it correct. Willoughby downed his mug and found it immediately refilled by an apologetic-looking Chambers. As he listened to the account of his own exploits, his confidence grew. It sounded bigger than life—his creeping through the woods in the predawn mist to leap upon enemy machine gun nests, he and his pals bayoneting a whole trench of Germans and making off with their Maxims. He had only been a corporal then. That little show got him promoted to sergeant and mentioned in dispatches. Yes, he was earning his stripes. Let Dunning put that in his pipe and smoke it.

Hmmm, must be the second cup of wine speaking. He'd never been much of a drinker, even after all those weeks in a platoon with Crawford and his gauche friends.

He hoped everyone was all right. The latest letter he'd received was from Major Thompson just a week ago, but so much could happen in a week. Plus he'd missed five days of mails thanks to the trip. Any urgent message about an injured friend would have missed him.

During his convalescence back in England he'd lost a few more friends. Hobbes and Moore had both been killed, and Watt had lost his sight in a blast. All of those had been school chums, and while he mourned them deeply they seemed to be part of a different life. His school days, although only six months past, hung faintly in his memory like some Elysian dream, some *Boy's Own* fantasy, an innocent childhood no one ever really had. It was the men in his regiment, men who he wouldn't have mingled with before the war and for the most part didn't even like, who he worried about most.

After the Germans had been pushed back at Ypres, the Oxs and Bucks had been pulled out of the line for a refit. They'd only been back at the front for a short time and Thompson's letters had said the sector was pretty quiet. Only a couple of men had been killed and both were strangers to him. Besides those, Edwards had contracted pneumonia but was said to be on the mend, and Crawford had gotten nicked by a sniper. A museum of minor wounds, that one. Always getting hurt but never in any serious way. Captain Cole had gotten hit by the same sniper, and that had been more serious. He was recovering in a hospital in Paris. His case wasn't bad enough to get shipped home, so Willoughby supposed he would be all right. He wondered who was Thompson's second-in-command while Cole was recovering.

Had anything else happened since he had last heard? Five days without mail was like not listening to a concert for five minutes. You lost track of the composition, perhaps even missed the end of the piece itself. He glanced at the entrance to the dugout. He really should be going.

"Show it to us, Willoughby."

The mention of his name brought his attention back to the men around the table. They were all looking at him. Ellis was giving him an expectant smile.

"I'm sorry, what?"

"Your knife. The one you got off that barbarian."

Willoughby stiffened.

"His name is Mustafa, and he and the other Colonials held the line at the Aisne with no help from the Frogs."

"Well, show it to us then."

In a fluid motion almost too quick to see, Willoughby leaned back, pushed his hand through the space left by an unbuttoned button on his greatcoat, grasped the hilt of the dagger hidden underneath, and whipped out his knife. Before his companions could even tell what it was, he'd hurled it down into the center of the table where it stood vibrating, the tip embedded in the wood, its keen blade shining in the candlelight.

Even Dunning looked impressed. Willoughby smiled. He'd had a lot of time to practice that maneuver while in hospital.

"It's called a *koummya*," Willoughby explained. "The traditional knife of Morocco. The Moroccans were holding the line next to us and they helped us on the raids Ellis mentioned. It was owned by a man named Abdullah Idrissi, who died fighting for France before I had the honor of meeting him. My friend Mustafa gave it to me."

Drake pulled it out of the wood and turned it over in his hands, testing the edge.

"Razor sharp, this. I can see how you could cut a Hun's throat with this bit of work."

The officers all passed it around and admired it. The two NCOs stopped their work at the stove to look at it too. The approving looks they gave him mattered more to Willoughby than the compliments from his school chums.

Ellis handed it back to him. He was about to point out where the Moors had carved his name in Arabic on the blade, but something held him back. He sheathed the weapon.

Another silence fell over the table, different this time. The men looked at him queerly, especially his old friends.

*Things have changed.*

Dunning produced a cigar. "Have a smoke?"

"Oh, Willoughby doesn't smoke," Drake said, laughing too quickly like he was breaking some tension he felt. But not Willoughby. He felt no more tension with these people.

"Bloody hell, he really is a socialist," Dunning grumbled.

"As a matter of fact I do smoke."

"Well doesn't war just change everything!" Drake laughed.

Drake's laughter was beginning to irritate him. These men laughed too easily. From a Christmas feast, a warm hearth, and gifts to. . .this. He'd rather be at home.

Dunning handed over the cigar and Ellis flicked open a lighter.

"Not now, thank you," Willoughby said, tucking the cigar into his pocket. He'd save it for one of the men. In truth he hadn't taken up smoking. He'd always thought it a vile habit and didn't believe the doctors when they said it was good for the health. How the blazes could inhaling smoke be good for you?

He wondered why he had lied, and then realized it had been the instinctive reaction of the enlisted man—never pass up something that could be useful. He had three packets of cigarettes in his pockets given to him by cheering civilians on the way here. He hadn't touched those either.

Willoughby lifted his mug, found it full once again of decent French wine. Who had filled it? He really shouldn't be drinking so much.

He raised the mug high.

"To the men on the line."

"To the men on the line," the officers around the table said, not catching his irony.

Willoughby drained his mug and stood up. He wavered and grasped the back of the chair. He really did need to learn how to hold his alcohol if he was going to survive this war.

"And now I must join them."

"Oh, but you just got here!" Ellis objected. "We're going to have a smashing dinner. We have two chickens freshly killed, some cakes and chocolates from home, and a bottle of bubbly I've been saving. The Oxs and Bucks can wait until tomorrow."

Willoughby smiled at his old friend. "No, I really must be going. Thank you for the hospitality."

"At least take some biscuits," Drake said, holding out a tin of Scottish shortbreads.

"Thank you," Willoughby said, stuffing them in his pocket.

Willoughby hefted his backpack, slung his rifle, and nearly fell as he stumbled out into the trench. His friends all bade him goodbye.

Willoughby sighed with relief as they disappeared into their dugout. "Back into it," he muttered.

He continued down the trench, munching on some shortbread and trying to remember the quartermaster's directions. It was beginning to grow dark. He'd have to hurry if he wanted to get there before nightfall. He didn't want to miss dinner.

The crowds were thinning out as men settled down to cook their meals in dugouts or support trenches. Only a few work parties were returning to the rear, having delivered whatever the high command had decided was fit for the men for a Christmas Eve dinner. The last issue of *The Times* he'd seen had boasted in a banner headline KITCHENER SENDS CHRISTMAS CHEER TO ARMY KITCHENS. He supposed that was meant to be witty. Willoughby didn't believe a word of it. The only joke was that whatever treats the Commander-in-Chief had sent, half would never make it, and the other half would be spoiled.

At least he was going forward.

Why had he been so tense back there? Why rush away when he had a warm spot and good food? Why had he done the same in Oxford?

Everyone in England had been so kind. Family and friends had streamed into the hospital in London bearing gifts. Mother had taken a hotel room on Regent Street so she could spend every day with him.

Father left his business and came down at least twice a week from Oxford, and his sisters were there any time they weren't in school.

After a month he was fit enough to return home to convalesce. He found the sitting room made up with streamers and a big banner his sisters had made saying WELCOME HOME. His meals were all his favorite dishes. Everyone beamed with pride and asked how he was healing. All he wanted to do was shut himself in his room.

Every day he waited anxiously for the postman in the hope that he'd get a letter from the front. On the days that one came, either in Thompson's tidy handwriting or Crawford's semiliterate scrawl, he'd hobble to his room and pore over the contents. On days when no letter came, he'd read every paper he could buy. Those never satisfied him. The "dispatches from the front" by "correspondents on the scene" all sounded like they'd been written in a Paris cafe. The *Oxford Mail* had a "Local Heroes" column with letters from men serving in France and Belgium. He even recognized some names from the Oxs and Bucks. All the tales were of the "chin up, stiff upper lip" variety, written by officers like the ones he had just left. None spoke the truth.

The worst was when Father brought his friends over. They'd break out the brandy and sit around the table, making Willoughby tell all his war stories. These middle-aged businessmen couldn't get enough of them. Well, if they admired war so much, why weren't they here? Age was no excuse. Major Thompson was fifty if he was a day. And from what he'd hard, the recruiters weren't so picky of late.

After a few drinks, his father, cheeks glowing like coals, would stand up and give a toast, "To the heroes of the front!"

Then Father would launch into one of his speeches. A few drams always produced a speech with him. Before the war it was The Yoke of the Gold Standard or The Demon of Socialism. These days it was The Barbarism of the German. The man positively hated Germans. Had never said a word against them before 1914, but now they were evil incarnate. He urged Willoughby to keep a running tally of the men he killed. At that point in the speech Willoughby usually begged off, saying he was feeling unwell.

"My boy is unaccustomed to drink," Father would explain to his cronies. "They stay clean out there in the trenches. Not a drop to be seen."

Willoughby would go back to his room. The being "unaccustomed to drink" part was true enough. At times he wished it wasn't. At times he envied the man who could drown his sorrows.

The shriek of an artillery shell tore him out of his memories and made him dive for the duckboard at his feet. The shell hit close, detonating with a loud bang. Shrapnel. Not so dangerous if you kept your head down. In the trenches the real danger was high explosive. If an HE shell hit close enough it would cave in a whole section of trench.

He'd nearly gotten buried once. The blast had torn loose a stretch of mud and clay ten feet long, knocking him off his feet and filling his mouth and ears. He'd been lucky. Several men had been buried. He'd pulled out Crawford with his own hands, pale and gasping but otherwise unhurt. Others had suffocated. They'd come out as cold and damp and lifeless as the clay itself.

Three more bangs in rapid succession told him the Germans were playing around only with shrapnel today. Bits of metal zipped and moaned overhead. The zipping ones were the balls that filled the inside of the shell casing, the moaners were larger fragments of the casing itself. What an education he was receiving. No one ever mentioned these tidbits of information in the *Oxford Mail,* and his tutors at Magdalen College skipped them during his lessons on Greek Philosophy and Elizabethan Theatre.

Willoughby kept his head down. The shells burst close, thumping their deadly cargo into the sandbags on the trench lip.

"Merry Christmas to you too, you fucking bastards!" Willoughby shouted.

Before the war he could have counted the number of times he had said "fuck" on one hand. Now it came naturally. It had even slipped out once at dinner. Mother had not been pleased.

As if in response, a shell burst in the air almost overhead. The duckboard shattered not five feet in front of him, hurtling splinters in all directions. Willoughby felt a tug at his pack.

He looked down at himself.

*Don't let me get injured just as I'm getting back.*

He patted himself down and found he was unhurt. There were several tears in his pack, however. Another explosion made him curl into a ball. He'd check what got damaged later.

Then, just as suddenly as it started, the bombardment stopped. Through ringing ears he heard someone screaming.

A man lay in the trench about fifteen feet in front of him, clutching his leg. Willoughby shucked off his pack and hurried over.

"I'm going to die! I'm going to die!" the man whimpered as blood seeped through his fingers.

He was a private of the First Lincolns. Judging from the newness of his kit he hadn't been out long.

"Let me see," Willoughby said as he knelt next to him.

"Careful, don't touch it!" the man shouted.

"Oh, don't be a baby. If you're shouting that loudly you can't be on death's door."

Willoughby pried the man's fingers away and saw a deep cut on the side of his leg just above the ankle. He unwound the man's puttees to see better. It didn't look serious. The blood was flowing, not spurting, so the shell splinter had missed the artery. Willoughby reached into the internal pocket under the right flap of the man's tunic where his field dressing would be. By strict orders everyone had to keep their field dressing in the same place. A rare bit of wisdom from High Command.

Opening the pack, he pulled out some cotton gauze and placed it on the cut.

"I'm bleeding to death!" the man shouted.

Willoughby took the man's hands and pressed them against the gauze.

"Keep direct pressure here and you won't. And do stop shouting."

Willoughby unspooled a long bandage and wound it around the man's leg, tying it off neatly.

The man sobbed, his breaths coming in panicked gusts. Willoughby slapped him across the face. The man jerked back and looked at him in astonishment.

Willoughby cradled the soldier's face in his hands and looked into his eyes.

"It's a scratch. You're not going to die. I've seen a lot worse and men pulled through. I've taken worse myself."

"R-really?"

Willoughby unbuttoned his greatcoat and his shirt underneath, exposing the bright red dot of a newly healed bullet wound.

"That got me a ticket home for two months."

The man's eyes widened. The sight seemed to reassure him.

"I-I'm going home?"

*More likely to that dressing station half a mile back, followed by two weeks light duty.*

"Paris at least."

The man looked disappointed. Two other soldiers of the First Lincolns hurried up.

"McKendrick, you all right?"

McKendrick grabbed Willoughby around the neck and hugged him.

"This chap saved my life!"

Willoughby buttoned up his shirt. He had successfully avoided this sort of scene through all his years at public school. It looked no better in a trench.

"I didn't save your life; I merely wrapped a cut you could have gotten just as easily in an English garden mishandling a hoe. Stop fondling me and have a cigar."

Willoughby shoved the cigar Dunning had given him into McKendrick's mouth. That shut him up. From a Christmas feast, a warm hearth, and gifts to. . .this.

Well, at least he was doing something useful.

"Thanks, mate," one of the other soldiers said, producing a match and lighting McKendrick's cigar.

"Take him back to the dressing station. I need to go."

Willoughby fetched his pack. The splinters had torn it in half a dozen places. Several jagged bits of metal had sliced through the top of the pack at an angle, missing the most precious contents in the middle. None of his food or other presents had been ruined, but he would have to put in to the regimental quartermaster for a new blanket and groundsheet. The pack he could mend himself with a bit of stitching. That was another thing he had learned in the army. The maid wasn't around to take care of these things.

He put on his pack and continued his journey. That near miss had cleared his head and he made better time. No more shells came over the wire. After a while he realized he didn't even hear any rifle fire. Perhaps the Germans wanted to settle in for a quiet Christmas Eve like everyone else. Some Prussian officer had probably gotten the idea to send over some shells to stir things up, but calmer heads over there had finally prevailed.

It looked like calmer heads prevailed on his side of No Man's Land too. The British batteries didn't respond like they usually did. If the Germans behaved themselves, it was all over for tonight.

That was fine by him. He was glad to be back—although he still couldn't exactly say why—but he didn't feel like getting killed on Christmas Eve.

Despite the quiet, he kept his shoulders hunched and his head low. He was getting close to the front. The trenches here were narrower, the men unshaven and dirty. People moved with care. Voices were muted. Sounds brought attention, and attention could bring mortar rounds. The Hun was past master at lobbing rounds over No Man's Land and straight into an active part of the British trench.

He came to an intersection and looked at the sign. He was still on Long Lane and branching off was Whizz Bang Way. That was a rather unpromising name. He'd just had some whizz bangs thrown at him back there with that booby from the First Lincolns. Unfortunately, this was the path he had to take.

The trench angled off towards the firing line. The quartermaster had told him it was the last communication trench he'd have to pass through before making it to the Oxs and Bucks. Another few minutes and he'd be home.

What? Had he actually thought that? Willoughby shook his head, adjusted his pack, and headed down Whizz Bang Way.

He soon saw why it was called that. The trench cut through a low swale. The sandbags on the parado had been shredded and torn by shrapnel. The top ends of the wooden supports were splintered and in some places lopped clean off. He stepped over a pool of fresh blood. If he had been foolish enough to peek over the parapet, he wagered he would see the German trench situated on a rise, with a clear view to this section of the line. Willoughby imagined they regularly hit this bit with their artillery. It was no wonder it was abandoned.

Still, it was the quickest way back to the lads, and it was getting dark. Willoughby picked up the pace.

He was getting close to the firing line now, he could feel it. The air felt like glass, ready to shatter all around him. There hung in it that tense silence that can only be produced by many men trying to keep quiet. He could hear that silence anywhere, so different than it was to typical lack of sound. It was something sensed, not heard.

He could smell that he was at the firing line too. That whiff of decay he'd passed a while back with the rats was twice as bad here. Every now and then he'd pass a bad stretch where some poor fellow lay just over the parapet, decaying in the mud as rats feasted on his innards.

Yes, and there were plenty of those vermin too. Always were close to where there had been fighting. He could see several scuttling along the duckboarding, or scrabbling up to the parapet to leave little footprints on the frosty sandbags.

*From a Christmas feast, a warm hearth, and gifts to a miserable ditch stinking of death. What a fool I am.*

He heard low voices ahead and caught a whiff of tobacco smoke. A sign hanging on the trench wall said, "TWENTY YARDS TO FIRING LINE. USE CAUTION." His heart lightened.

Whizz Bang Way opened onto the firing line trench. It was narrower and deeper than the support trenches. Men sat on the fire step chatting and smoking. For a moment he stopped and stared. All those hunched and tired men wrapped in greatcoats, some with blankets around them like shawls to keep out the cold, laughing and joking, their filthy faces wreathed with smiles. Willoughby let out a sigh of relief and felt his tension fade.

One wall of the trench was pierced at regular intervals with the dark openings of dugouts. A familiar face emerged from one.

"Fisher!" Willoughby called out.

The private turned and his face lit up.

"Well Lord bless us, it's Willoughby back from hospital!"

The private ran over and embraced him. Willoughby smiled even though the hug made his side twinge. No salutes here.

Everyone turned to look. He called out to Black and Hedges and Robertson and they gathered around. He saw a lot of unfamiliar faces as well. Too many. The year had not been kind to his regiment.

"What you doin' back here?" Black demanded. "Shouldn't you be at home sporting with the girls?"

"They declared me fit for service."

"Who, the Army or the girls?" Black said with a smile.

"Fit for service?" a familiar voice called out. "Oi, there's a laugh!"

Private Emmet Crawford pushed his way through the crowd. He booted a newcomer from where he was sitting on the fire step.

"You, whatsyourname, I'm on sentry duty in fire bay four. Get your dirty arse over there and take my place."

The man grabbed his Lee-Enfield and scuttled off.

Crawford strode up to Willoughby, a gap-toothed grin spreading across his face.

"Well look what the cat dragged in."

Willoughby scowled at him. "I should have you brought up on charges for not properly addressing a superior officer. You'll be in the brigade guardhouse where you belong before dinner."

Several of the newcomers snapped to attention.

Willoughby and Crawford laughed. Crawford grabbed him by the lapels.

"Jesus fucking Christ, save me from these tenderfeet!"

Willoughby laughed again and gave him a playful slap upside the head. It was good to be back.

"So how is everyone?" Willoughby asked, anxiously looking around to spot as many familiar faces as he could.

"We wrote you about Cole. He's still in hospital but on the mend. Did you get my note about Sangster?"

"Who?"

"New bloke. I wrote you a few days ago but I guess the post missed you."

"I didn't know him. Was he one of the reserves?"

"Yeah. A subaltern attached to Brigade as a translator. Bit of a linguist like you. Spoke French and German as well as you do."

"Did he?" Willoughby couldn't help but feel jealous. His language skills had given him a privileged position in Thompson's Company E.

"The Brigadier sent him over as Cole's temporary replacement. Made for a good liaison with the Belgians and helped out with the questioning of a prisoner we grabbed."

"Crawford's fists did most of the talking!" Black laughed.

"Charming. So how did Sangster meet his end?" Willoughby asked.

"Stuck his nose above the parapet to have a look around," Crawford said, turning to scowl along the trench and raising his voice. "Why don't these new ones keep their bally heads down?"

"We need steel helmets," MacDonald said, striding up. He was the company medical man and sported a Red Cross armband. "I can't count the number of times I've written to High Command about it. They never reply. Good to see you Willoughby."

"Perhaps you should write the *Oxford Mail*," Willoughby said with a bitter smile as he shook the regimental doctor's hand. Willoughby raised an eyebrow. The man wasn't in uniform.

Crawford caught his look. "Oh, you didn't hear. Good old Magnetic MacDonald was being a bit more magnetic than usual last Tuesday. A high explosive round went off right by him and tore all his clothes off!"

Everyone laughed. MacDonald had an eerie talent for close scrapes. As usual, he seemed to have come out of it with nothing hurt but his dignity.

"Poor Sangster," Black sighed as he shook his head. "He'll never make it to Spain now."

"Spain?"

"Yeah, he was teaching himself Spanish from a little book. Said he wanted to move there."

"Whatever for, to be a bullfighter?" Willoughby asked.

"Who knows? He should have gone while he had the chance. He'd have a wine glass in his hand and some dusky lass on his lap. Instead he'd taking a permanent nap in six feet of Flanders mud, the bloody fool."

"Stand to!" a harsh voice shouted down the line.

Crawford rolled his eyes. "New Captain here while Cole tussles with the nurses. Bit of a wanker."

Men scattered to take their places on the fire step. It was almost sunset, and with the sun silhouetting anyone peering over the parapet, it the perfect time for the Germans to launch an attack. Everyone fixed bayonets and checked their magazines. Only one man per section had to actually look over the parapet, but everyone else had to be ready in case of trouble. Willoughby took his place between Crawford and Fisher and rested his head against a sandbag. Not far off, Black took sentry duty, keeping his head low.

Faint sounds of German commands and rattling bayonets told him the enemy was standing to as well. With the sun in their eyes, it was a good time for the British to attack too. The roles were reversed in the morning, when everyone had to stand-to before breakfast.

"Seem to be keeping down," Black reported.

A stern-faced older man with captain's stripes on his sleeve strode along the line.

"You there, adjust that ammunition pouch. And you, don't slouch so."

Crawford spat. Willoughby studied the captain and silently agreed with Crawford's assessment.

The captain strode up to Willoughby, face reddening.

"And who are you?"

"Sergeant Willoughby returning from medical leave and reporting for duty, sir," he replied with a salute. No one saluted at stand-to because of the risk of accidentally lifting your hand over the parapet, but Willoughby had the impression this fellow didn't know that and wouldn't care even if he did.

"Very well, as you were." The captain gave a curt nod and walked away.

"Nice to meet you too," Willoughby muttered as the officer disappeared around the turn leading to the next fire bay. Crawford grinned.

"When did you say Cole gets back?" Willoughby asked.

"Not a moment too soon," Crawford grumbled.

"Still no movement," Black reported.

"I got a movement," Hedges called out. "Captain Kaiser called stand-to just as I was undoing me trousers!"

The whole fire bay erupted in laughter.

"That was a bit bold even for Hedges," Willoughby said. "If the captain hears that he'll be up for a week's fatigue duty."

"Deaf as a post, the man is," Fisher said. "Got hit by a shell at the Marne. Blasted naked like poor Magnetic MacDonald and lost most of his hearing in the bargain."

"So now you're going to tell me that he shouts because he's deaf and as good Christians we should think more kindly of him," Willoughby said. Fisher got a lot of ribbing from being a member of the God Squad.

"No, he was probably shouting like that since his poor mother weaned him," Fisher said. "The Good Lord sends us wankers in order to test our faith."

Everyone erupted in laughter again.

"*Die Tommies haben riesigen Spaß dabei!*" a shout came from No Man's Land.

Black ducked down and looked to Willoughby.

"What the hell did he say?"

"He said the Tommies are having a lot of fun," Willoughby translated.

"Well if they want us to have more fun how about they take the captain?" Crawford said.

"Let's send him over!" Willoughby agreed.

A hand rested on Willoughby's shoulder. He turned and saw the smiling face of Major Thompson, commander of Company E.

Willoughby blushed. He surely must have heard.

"Good to see you, Willoughby, how are you?" his commander asked, neither demanding a salute nor giving any indication that he had heard the men's jibes.

"Better, sir," Willoughby said.

"Pity you missed Christmas at home by a whisker."

*Not a pity at all, sir.*

Willoughby felt a bit guilty. His family was all right. Father was a bit of a blowhard but loved him as a father should. Always wanted the best for him and worked hard to provide it. And Mother and his two sisters were wonderful. Their letters sustained him when he was at the front, but for some reason when he was in Oxford spending every day with them, all he could think about was getting back here.

Thompson took his silence for regret. He patted Willoughby on the shoulder.

"Well, don't worry. We're having a bit of a do here at the front. Quite a heap of mail came up, and some treats in the rations too."

"I've brought a fair number myself, sir. They'll be making the rounds."

"Good lad. I'd best see to the next section."

Thompson headed out.

"What did you bring?" Crawford asked.

"Some cake my mother made, mountains of chocolate, and two bottles of Scotch."

"Bloody hell, you're like an overeducated Santa Claus!"

"I have presents too. Except for you, of course. You get coal."

Willoughby reached into his pocket, pulled out a lump of coal, and tossed it to him. The fire bay erupted in laughter. Willoughby joined in. He'd been waiting weeks to pull off that stunt.

"You bloody bastard," Crawford said, punching him on the shoulder.

Captain "Kaiser"—Willoughby still hadn't learned his real name and decided it didn't matter—stormed around the turn of the traverse.

"Men, just because it's a holiday in happier places doesn't mean there's room for levity on the firing line!" he barked.

"*Schweinhund, lassen Sie sie lachen!*" a call came from over No Man's Land. The captain didn't hear.

"You men must have proper comportment while on duty," the captain lectured. With that he spun on his heel and disappeared around the traverse again.

"I thought you said he was as deaf as a post?" Willoughby grumbled.

"Not to insubordination he isn't," Crawford replied.

"What did that shouting mean?" Black asked as he looked over the parapet.

"It means someone over there understands English," Willoughby replied.

"Fine, but what did he say?"

"He called the captain a pig dog and told him to let us laugh if we want to."

"Oi, the Hun's not all bad," Crawford grinned.

"*Meine freunde sage du bist eine gut Mann!*" Willoughby called out.

"*Danke!*"

Crawford's eyes went wide. "Steady. That's comporting with the enemy."

"The word is 'consorting', and since when were you a stickler for rules?"

"Not saying that, but still."

Willoughby shrugged. He didn't know what had come over him. He felt giddy being back with his old friends, but Crawford was right, talking to a Hun was a bit much. There'd been the occasional exchange of insults when they were dug in at the Aisne and Ypres, but getting chatty was well out of order.

Crawford held up the coal. "I'm going to light this under your bunk when you're asleep."

"Very funny. That reminds me, I need to get a blanket and groundsheet. Mine got shredded by the Germans' Christmas Eve greetings."

"You can have Sangster's. His things haven't gone back yet. They should burn nicely," Crawford said with a wicked grin.

"If I go up in flames I won't be able to give you your Christmas present."

Crawford's eyebrows went up. "You got me something?"

"You and some of the other lads. All the gang."

"What did you bring?"

"You'll see."

"Come on."

"Wait. We're supposed to be prepared to resist the enemy."

"They aren't coming over."

"They had better not. I'm still a bit nettled about that shrapnel. I had to patch up some new man who got all panicky at the sight of a few drops of blood."

Crawford shook his head. "This new lot aren't the same quality as the veterans."

"Sad but true," Fisher said. "They've used up all the Army and Reserves, and now it's all new men."

Willoughby sighed. Two months ago Fisher, who had been in the Reserves, had been considered a new man. But he was right. At least the Reserves had training. These new men had been packed off to training camps for a couple of months of drill, and then rushed into the line. That sad show with the wounded chap in the support trench would have never happened with a Reservist. From the letters Crawford and the others sent, it seemed ten of the new men died for every one of the old set. Not that there were many of the old set left.

Suddenly Willoughby had a terrible vision. It was of a conveyor belt like they had in those new factories. Instead of hats or cans of soup, it was moving along men, a steady line of men being stamped, prodded, and packaged as soldiers and then sent to market. He'd seen the recruitment centers back home. They were brimming with volunteers, many of whom looked like they were lying about their age. But what happened when the eagerness wore off? There were already signs of that. The dense typeface of the fatality pages in the daily papers was having an effect. So what happened when they stopped rushing to the recruitment office?

*Conscription. That's what. So instead of eager fools they'll have uneager ones. And more deaths.*

*God, the Germans must be in the same fix too. And the Turks and the French and the Russians and everyone else who's leaping into this war. Will everyone have long conveyor belts of men, chomping and chomping until God knows when?*

"You all right?" Fisher asked.

"Being back takes a bit of getting used to."

Fisher smiled. "You should have tried to stay home. You've earned a bit more rest time."

Willoughby shook his head. Fisher gave him a queer look and Willoughby turned away.

Crawford slapped him on the back. "Chin up. We're getting a feast tonight. And a bit of your father's Scotch will set things right."

"As long as Captain Kaiser doesn't pinch it," Black grumbled as he looked through the periscope.

"No chance of that," Fisher said. "I'm sure Thompson will keep him well in hand. You'll be able to sully your minds with alcohol all night if you wish."

Willoughby jabbed a thumb in Fisher's direction. "Good to have a teetotaler in the ranks, he can stand watch."

Everyone chuckled, even Fisher. Thompson strode down the line.

"Stand down!" he ordered. "All right men, the kitchen party is just coming up. Let's eat."

Everyone but the sentries got off the fire step. There was a rattle down the line as the men removed their bayonets from the ends of their rifles and sheathed them. Soon Willoughby was back to the familiar bustle around the trenches. Men shuffled around each other as they retrieved their mess kits and prepared to eat. The waft of cooked meat passed through the air. As crowded and stinking as the front line trenches were, you could always smell the mess party before you saw it.

"Here, I'll show you our dugout," Crawford said. There was no invitation to bunk with the old crowd. None was needed.

Crawford led him to a tiny hole in the front wall of the trench. Worming their way inside, they entered a small version of the dugout where Willoughby had been invited to drinks. It was a simple cyst in the earth, with three thick logs holding up the roof and duckboarding on the floor and room for six men to sleep side by side. A niche in the wall held a candle. There was no other furniture.

"So what did you get me?" Crawford asked as Willoughby set out his things in the narrow space provided him.

"Quit pestering me, it's not even Christmas yet. Not much space in here, is there?"

"Hope you don't turn in your sleep, otherwise we'll all have to turn at the same time."

Willoughby grinned. "Let's eat."

As they emerged from the dugout they found Thompson waiting for them.

Now that he wasn't on watch, Willoughby was able to salute.

"We've long since dispensed with such formalities," Thompson said with a smile.

"We're all mucking about in the same muddy hole with rats and lice, he means!" Crawford said.

"Is there anything I can do for you, sir?" Willoughby asked.

"I just wanted to give you a quick tour. Crawford, come along, you have eyes as sharp as your tongue. Shan't take a minute. You won't miss dinner."

Thompson led them along the line to a narrow cutting that, instead of heading back to the support trenches, led out into No Man's Land. It was blocked by a steel plate and guarded by a sentry. As the sentry pulled the plate aside, the major drew his pistol and got on his hands and knees. Crawford drew a Luger that he had obviously filched from an enemy corpse and handed it to Willoughby.

"These are more manageable where we're going," he explained.

"What will you carry?" Willoughby asked, looking over the unfamiliar weapon.

Crawford grinned and drew a small automatic from the pocket of his greatcoat. Willoughby recognized it as a Savage Model 1907.

"You remember this, don't you? Albert gave it to me. That poor Frog is out of the war thanks to a shattered wrist. Sent me his two pistols by parcel post. Keep your eyes open. We don't man the observation trench during the day. Too exposed. But I wouldn't put it past the Hun to stick a man or two in there to give us a nasty surprise. Our side aren't the only ones putting out raiding parties."

"The Hun's doing it now too?" Willoughby asked.

"Yes, and doing it well," Major Thompson said. "One group especially."

The two men slung their rifles and started crawling forward on their knees and elbows, pistols at the ready.

"This gets a bit shallow in spots," Thompson explained with a whispered warning.

The trench led out fifty yards into No Man's Land. The stench of death was greater here, barely cut by the crisp air. As they worked their way forward, the friendly, familiar sounds of their front line faded and they were blanketed in a tense hush. All they heard was a strong breeze making the barbed wire hum. Willoughby also caught the faint sound of flapping cloth. A flag? No, there were no flags here. A greatcoat, more likely, or a tattered bit of shirt, worn by some dead Englishman or German hanging on the wire.

In a quiet, distant corner of his mind, Willoughby realized that this was the most relaxed he had been since he had been shot two months before. In the dressing station there had been pain and terror. In the hospital there had been a wordless emptiness that had deepened the healthier he became. By the time he was hobbling around his old neighborhood in Oxford he was going half mad with distraction. Every conversation with family and neighbors a silent clash, every social call a grinding burden.

His first weeks in the war had been ones of exhaustion and fear—fear of the enemy, but more so fear of what the others thought of him. Tough men like Crawford and Cole and Black, men who worked with their hands and had fought all their lives, whether against the Hun or some thug in a pub. But he had fought too, and had fought well. He had earned their respect by charging the enemy on feet bloodied by weeks of hard marching, earned their respect by defeating Germans twice his size with nothing but a knife. He had saved friends' lives, and had been saved by them in turn. He was still the odd man out, but he was no longer an outsider.

He had thought of Oxford and the university as heaven on earth, and yet had never been comfortable there, always being ill at ease that some other chap would prove to be the better scholar. Now that he was in the midst of hell on earth, he had found his place.

All this ran through his mind half-consciously, a background thought as his eyes focused on every declivity of the trench wall, ears perked for any strange sound. Thompson's warning had been sound. The trench was too exposed to crossfire to dig properly and in places was barely two feet deep. Willoughby prayed the Germans didn't decide to shell it. While the back of his mind wondered at the strange turn his life had taken, his foremost thoughts were of staying alive.

Crawling forward as quietly as they could, they eventually made it to the end of the trench, a simple shell hole blasted into the earth some months before. It had been shored up with sandbags here and there, but it remained essentially a shell hole. The bottom was taken up by a frozen puddle, brown with mud. To one side lay a shredded boot. The white line of a weathered bone was visible through the tear. Willoughby barely glanced at it. Such sights had long since stopped bothering him.

Edging around the inside of the crater, careful not to step on the puddle and give away their position by cracking the ice, Thompson got to the side closest to the German line. Willoughby and Crawford flanked him. Both men put away their pistols and unslung their rifles.

Thompson pulled out a small periscope, its top daubed with clay and festooned with sticks and a muddy bit of old sock, and eased it over the lip of the crater. He stared through the viewer for a minute and then indicated that Willoughby should take over.

Willoughby looked out over the devastation of No Man's Land. Life in a trench was a life of narrow spaces. It was rare to look over the parapet unless one was on sentry duty. What Willoughby saw sunk his spirits. The fifty yards or so between this forward observation post and the enemy trench—clearly visible by its double row of barbed wire and heap of sandbags—was a surreal landscape of shell craters, bodies, rats, and the blackened stumps of trees.

How much of a difference two months could make! When he had been stationed not far from here in October, the land had been pockmarked with craters but many of the trees still stood, and grass or the stubble of wheat stuck up between the ugly marks left by artillery. Even a forlorn house or two, its walls cracked and roof burnt away, still stood between the lines. No more. He saw no farmhouses, no grass, no tree or bush that still lived. Two months of artillery bombardments and charges had churned up the soil into this muddy hellscape, now frozen by the chill of the Belgian winter into a jagged spread of brownish gray through which nothing moved but rats.

The next thing he noticed was the source of that flapping noise. The remains of a British Tommy hung on the German wire, probably marking the furthest point reached by some ill-fated charge. The greatcoat and trousers appeared deflated, as the flesh beneath had all but disappeared. Withered hands whose fingers were held on only by rotted ligaments scraped the cold ground, and one half of the coat waved like a banner in the breeze.

He turned the periscope to scan the German trench.

There wasn't much to see. The parapet was rough from where shell blasts had caved it in and the Germans had shored it up. In places there were sandbags smeared with mud. He spotted one cluster of sandbags that surrounded a narrow space from which poked the muzzle of a Maxim machine gun. A little to the left he spotted another cluster of sandbags, with a steel barrier that looked like a small version of the one that sealed off the end of the observation trench. It had a small hole pierced into it, just large enough for a man to fire through and see where he was shooting.

*If we had some bombs we could probably get rid of those from here. Why doesn't the High Command hurry up and issue more?*

At least they had enough artillery shells these days. Back in the early months of the war the British guns went silent half the time for lack of ammunition.

*We'll get our grenades in time, as will the Germans. And then what? Then we'll have to invent new tactics, and then we'll each create newer weapons to defeat the new tactics, and the conveyor belt will continue to roll.*

He finished his survey, noting breaks in the wire and spots where the terrain would allow them to approach closer to the enemy position than in other spots. Without realizing it, he was already back in the mindset of the front. He was already planning his next raid. He didn't even have to ask if there would be one. The Oxs and Bucks had become famous for their raids.

Willoughby withdrew the periscope and handed it back to Major Thompson. He nodded and without a word they wormed their way back to the British trench.

"So tell me about this German raiding party," Willoughby said once they made it back and the sentry had pushed the steel barrier into place.

"We haven't had a good look at them," Major Thompson said. "They strike along various spots on the line and have only hit us once."

"So how do you know they are the same group?" Willoughby asked.

"Because they're too damn good," Crawford grunted. "It's a small group, five or six men. One's a buck Hun that would have put old Saunders to shame. Another is an older fellow, probably the commander although they don't wear any badges. Has a big handlebar moustache."

"So you've seen them? How do you know about the badges?" Willoughby asked, feeling a tug of sadness at hearing the name of an old comrade, now buried.

"When they hit us just before dawn one day we got into it with them," Crawford said. "I got a glance at the older fellow before he nearly blew my head off with his pistol. I hate to say this, but when I dodged all that did was put the bullet into the man behind me."

"These things happen, private, it's not your fault," Thompson said.

"Never said it was, just gets on my tits, it does."

"Eloquently put," Thompson said. "We managed to kill one before they slunk off. The body had no papers or distinguishing badges. It's a clever idea and we've adopted it. We have to watch out for these chaps. That raid wrecked a Vickers gun and killed three of our lads. The raids on other regiments were even more successful."

"Competition," Willoughby grunted. "It was only a matter of time before the enemy imitated our methods."

"They're a sneaky bunch," Crawford said. "I wouldn't be surprised if they gave us a Christmas present. The Major's ordered double sentries."

"Barbarians," Willoughby grumbled.

"Well, that's enough war for one evening," Thompson said. "Get something to eat and hopefully the night will pass with no trouble. I've sent Captain Dickson back to the Brigade Quartermaster to see to a few things. He shouldn't be back for at least an hour."

Crawford and Willoughby smiled and nodded. They knew what their commander meant by that. Willoughby returned to the dugout to retrieve his Scotch.

They found the rest of the men seated around a few steaming dixies. Willoughby could smell beef stew, hot tea, and potato soup. There was also a small crate full of butter cookies that had obviously been brought up from the regimental quartermaster stores rather than someone's private mail.

They ate their fill and sneaked a few drinks as well. When the conversation flagged, they could hear the Germans enjoying their meal not far off. Laughter and jokes in German filtered across No Man's Land.

Willoughby yawned. He leaned against the trench wall and closed his eyes.

"You never could handle your liquor," Crawford laughed.

"I'm just tired."

"Turn in, then, and dream of Saint Nick and Christmas roast."

Willoughby shook his head. "I never dream when I'm out here."

"Who does?" Black snorted. "We're all too damn tired."

"Must you blaspheme even on the eve of our Lord's birth?" Fisher grumbled.

"It's not just that," Willoughby said. "Even on rest periods I don't dream. Remember after the Aisne?"

"Two whole days in billets, that was fine!" Crawford said.

"Twelve hours sleep the first night, and ten the night after, if I remember correctly," Willoughby said. "Yet even then I didn't dream."

Crawford studied him. "Did you dream when you were back home?"

"You mean in England? Yes."

"About what?" Fisher asked.

Willoughby looked at the men around him. "I dreamt about being back here."

***

The next morning, Willoughby woke up to singing.

He put on his greatcoat and poked his head out of the dugout. The trench walls glittered with frost. Men stamped their feet and kept their hands in their pockets, their breath coming out in white plumes. Three red-nosed men stood nearby singing "Jingle Bells" and holding mugs of what obviously wasn't tea. Black strolled by and Willoughby grabbed him.

"What happened to stand to?" Willoughby asked.

"You slept through it."

"You should have woken me. Captain Kaiser will have me in irons!"

"Special order from the major. Consider it a Christmas present."

"Christmas? Oh, right."

Black extended a hand, "Merry Christmas."

"Merry Christmas," Willoughby replied, shaking it.

"Come on, you missed breakfast too, but we saved you some. Fisher got a spirit stove from home. We can test it out reheating your tea."

They found their circle of friends in the next fire bay huddled around Fisher's new spirit stove. Everyone greeted him and passed him a cup of tea.

"Plenty for everyone," Fisher said. "The captain made himself useful for once and came back with extra."

As Willoughby took a steaming cup, Crawford leaned over and tipped his flask over it.

"A bit early, isn't it?" Willoughby chuckled.

"No it isn't," Crawford said. "So where's my present?"

"I'll go back and get my pack."

"Nonsense," Crawford said, and turning to one of the new men shouted, "You, whatsyourname, go get the sergeant's pack!"

"Yes, sir," the man said, scuttling off.

"You have them eating out of your hand."

"A tot of rum and a boot to the rear and they all dance to my tune. Carrot and stick method, it's called."

"You'll make general one day."

"Jesus Christ, no!" Crawford said in mock terror. "Oh, we have something for you. While you were drinking pints and watching the cricket back home, we managed to have some laughs too. We got a whole week rest period in Gay Paree. Ah, you should have been there! Wine, women, song, women. Did I say women twice? Well, never mind. One day at a kiosk I saw these and thought of you. Here's your gift," Crawford said as he handed him a thin envelope.

"Demobilization papers?" Willoughby asked.

"You wish!" Crawford laughed.

Fisher got up from the circle and walked away grumbling.

"Never mind him, open it," Crawford said.

Willoughby opened the envelope and pulled out a stack of photos. The first was of a French woman with one leg on a chair and her skirts hiked up. As the circle of men snickered, Willoughby shuffled through the photos and found they were all of a similar nature.

"I'll. . .treasure these."

"Just don't treasure them in the dugout," Black said. "I don't want to get hit by a stray!"

"This is what I missed while I was on sick leave—the refined conversation, the highbrow intellectual rigor of the trenches."

"Oi, don't you like my gift?"

Willoughby pulled out a picture of a nude dancer with breasts bigger than her head.

"Well. . ."

"And that's only the first part of the gift," Crawford said. "The lads felt bad that you were missing out on the fun—"

"Michelle, sweet Michelle," Black sighed.

"Especially her. So we decided that we would treat you next time we're in Paris. We'll all pitch in. Otherwise you might as well convert to Catholicism and become a monk. You'll never get a tumble on your own."

"We agreed to pitch in? I don't remember that," Hedges said. His face was already red, and not from the cold.

"You were drunk."

"And you weren't?"

"Of course I was. We were in Paris, you bloody idiot."

The private returned with his pack and Willoughby quickly changed the subject by presenting the gifts he had brought.

"Aha! The hour of reckoning is at hand!" Black said.

"Which reminds me, I have something for Fisher. Hello, Fisher! Come back. They're done being boors and it's time to get your gift."

Willoughby handed out packages to all his friends—socks, gloves, cigarettes, chocolates, all the little things they needed and the Army didn't provide, or didn't provide in sufficient quality or quantity. He saved Crawford for last. Out of the corner of his eye he could see him shifting impatiently like a child. Finally Willoughby handed him a large, soft package wrapped in paper.

Crawford tore it open and pulled out a hand-knit sweater.

"Oi, this is tops, mate. Just what I needed. Hey, perfect size too. Cheers."

"It's not from me, read the note attached."

"Not from you?" Crawford asked as he pulled out a little envelope from the shredded wrapping.

"It's from my sister."

"Ooooooh!" all the men rolled their eyes.

"You mean Sarah? Eighteen years old and still unmarried. Glad to have her knitting for me."

"No, it's from Betsy, my younger sister. She's ten so she's too young for you in addition to being too good for you."

"There's the pity, but it's a nice sweater in any case."

"Well, read the note," Black said.

"Give him a moment, he's not good at such things," Willoughby said.

"Watch it," Crawford said, and held up the note to the light.

*Dear Mr. Crawford—Mister, that's a laugh!—My brother says you don't get any packages from home so I knitted you this sweater. It took me six weeks to finish for I do not have much time between school and helping out with the Girl Guides baking biscuits for the men at the front. Hugh got your measurements and sent them to me just before he was hit. Do take care of him and make sure he is careful. He's awfully silly at times—bloody right!—and is liable to get hurt again. Please send me your foot size so I can knit you some socks next. And do write me if you want to hear from England I am happy to write you. There is a tin of Girl Guide biscuits in Hugh's pack for you as well. I know you will share them with the men. Hugh says you only pretend to be selfish. Take care and write me and don't forget to tell me your sock size. Merry Christmas, Betsy Willoughby."*

Nobody spoke for a moment. Crawford passed a hand over his eyes, muttered something Willoughby didn't catch, and walked away. Briefly Willoughby wondered if he should follow him and decided against it. Part of friendship is knowing when not to be there.

The distant sound of singing caught his ear. The others heard it too and perked up. It was coming across No Man's Land.

*"O Tannenbaum, o Tannenbaum,*
*Wie treu sind deine Blätter!*
*Du grünst nicht nur zur*
*Sommerzeit,*
*Nein, auch im Winter, wenn es*
*schneit.*
*O Tannenbaum, o Tannenbaum,*
*Wie treu sind deine Blätter!"*

Willoughby's heart lightened and he stood up.

"That sounds like 'O Christmas Tree,'" Black said.

"That's because it is," Willoughby said. He stepped over to the parapet and, while taking care not to put his head into view, cupped his hands around his mouth and sang out in a loud voice,

*"O Christmas tree, O Christmas tree!*

*How are thy leaves so verdant!*
*Not only in the summertime, But even in winter is thy prime.*
*O Christmas tree, O Christmas tree,*
*How are thy leaves so verdant!"*

"Oi, you sound like a strangled cat," Black laughed.

"Can you do better?" Willoughby asked with a grin.

Black stood up beside him and belted out in a surprisingly sweet voice,

*"O Christmas tree, O Christmas tree,*
*Much pleasure dost thou bring me!*
*For ev'ry year the Christmas tree, Brings to us all both joy and glee.*
*O Christmas tree, O Christmas tree,*
*Much pleasure dost thou bring me!"*

A reply came from over the parapet.

*"O Tannenbaum, o Tannenbaum,*
*Du kannst mir sehr gefallen!*
*Wie oft hat nicht zur Weihnachtszeit*
*Ein Baum von dir mich hoch erfreut!*
*O Tannenbaum, o Tannenbaum,*
*Du kannst mir sehr gefallen!*

Willoughby and Black smiled at each other and sang out together,

*"O Christmas tree, O Christmas tree—"*

"What's all this!" Captain Dickson stormed down the trench. "Stop that singing this instant!"

"We're just singing carols, sir," Black said.

"You're consorting with the enemy, and if you do it again I'll have you up on charges."

*"Verpiss dich, Miststück!"*

The captain looked uncertainly at the parapet. Willoughby coughed in order to hide his laughter. He turned as Fisher began to sing in a soft voice.

*"Silent night, holy night,*

*All is calm, all is bright,*
*Round yon Virgin Mother and Child,*
*Holy Infant so tender and mild,*
*Sleep in heavenly peace,*
*Sleep in heavenly peace"*

Fisher looked up at the captain. "Germans can't hear if I sing this low, sir."

The captain's eyes narrowed. He grunted and stalked away. As soon as he was around the corner Fisher started again in a loud, clear voice.

*"Silent night, holy night,*
*All is calm, all is bright,*
*Round yon Virgin Mother and Child,*
*Holy Infant so tender and mild,*
*Sleep in heavenly peace,*
*Sleep in heavenly peace"*

Willoughby looked on in wonder. Fisher never broke the rules.

An answer came over No Man's Land.

*"Stille Nacht, Heilige Nacht,*
*Alles schläft; einsam wacht,*
*Nur das traute heilige Paar,*
*Holder Knab im lockigten Haar,*
*Schlafe in himmlischer Ruh!*
*Schlafe in himmlischer Ruh!"*

Fisher continued onto the next verse, and out past the wire the German sang in his own language, but in unison.

Other men in both trenches joined in. After another couple of lines Willoughby did too. Captain Dickson came storming around the corner with Major Thompson just behind. Everyone sang louder.

The captain started shouting for them to stop but cut off short as Major Thompson put a restraining hand on his shoulder. Willoughby couldn't hear what the major said over his own singing, but the captain objected loudly, face going red. Thompson glared at him and barked something back. The captain stiffened and snapped out a salute before beating a hasty retreat.

Willoughby and several others missed the next verse as they snickered. Thompson rarely pulled rank on a subordinate unless it was some slothful quartermaster who was responsible for not feeding the men on time. To see him do it to his second-in-command was a Christmas present to be cherished.

The song finished, replaced with a hush. Men looked at each other. Thompson had a strange look in his eye, a mixture of pride and deep sadness.

*"Kameraden!"*

Private Black went to the periscope and looked through.

"Blimey! Would you look at that?"

Thompson went over and looked through the eyepiece.

"They have a Christmas tree over there," he said with a smile.

Everyone rushed to the parapet. Some crowded around the periscope. A few men poked their heads above the parapet. Willoughby grabbed the nearest one and pulled him back.

"Keep down, you fool!"

"It's all right, sergeant!" a man further down the line said. His had his head and shoulders fully exposed. He wasn't the only one.

"Get down, that's an order!" Thompson said.

The men crouched down. Someone produced another periscope and Willoughby looked through it. Sure enough, a small Christmas tree, complete with tinsel and a little angel on top, was poking up over the German lines, not far from the Maxim gun.

Their machine gun looked strange. Willoughby squinted and realized there was mistletoe stuck in the barrel.

The Germans started singing again, this time a carol nobody recognized. That it was a carol wasn't in question. It had that joyous, pure air to it, that sound of a well-remembered song from childhood for which everyone knows the words.

The soldiers in the British trench stood still and listened. After the Germans were done, Willoughby heard Crawford's voice ring out.

"Hey, Huns! Merry Christmas!"

A heavily accented response came from the other side of the wire. "Merry Christmas to you too, Tommy!"

"Oi, someone speaks English over there," Crawford laughed. "Hey, Hun! The name's Crawford! We're not all named Tommy you know."

"My name is Hans! Merry Christmas to you too, Crawford."

Crawford hoisted himself up on the parapet, exposing the top half of his body. He was wearing the sweater Betsy had knitted him.

Willoughby hurried over to him.

"What in blazes are you doing?"

"It's Christmas. The Hun isn't going to shoot."

"You're going to take that on faith?" Willoughby pulled at him. Crawford was much stronger and stayed where he was.

"Got any beer over there, Hans?" Crawford called out.

"*Ja.* You have any Scotch whiskey?"

Willoughby peeked over the parapet. Three German soldiers were sitting on their own parapet, fully visible to the British line.

Not far from him, Willoughby heard the muttered line, "This is too good an opportunity to miss."

He spun around and saw a British soldier take aim with his rifle. Willoughby slapped the man upside the head.

"Put down that rifle, that's an order!" he said in a harsh whisper.

The man gaped at him.

"Since when don't we shoot at Huns?"

"Since right now."

The man's face turned red. "I lost a good pal just last week and you're telling me—"

"That's enough, private," Thompson's voice sounded behind them. "Do as you're ordered and put down your rifle."

The man stared at the major in amazement, but did as he was told.

Major Thompson's tone softened. "If you had fired, what do you think would have happened to Crawford? Is that the way you want to spend Christmas?"

The man hung his head. "No, sir."

Willoughby watched all this with a growing fascination. A queer feeling came over him, strengthened by a sudden resolve. He grasped the wooden support post on the trench wall and hauled himself over the parapet.

No Man's Land and the German trench came into view. A half dozen Germans were visible poking their heads or upper bodies above their own defense. It seemed closer than before. The earth bit into his knees as he got atop the parapet.

He stood up in full view of the enemy line, letting out a gust of breath as he did so.

The Germans stared openmouthed. He turned and looked back at his pals down in the trench, all those astonished faces looking up at him, Major Thompson too stunned to even shout.

*How small they look. This is why I do this. Back home I'm small. Here I'm a giant. In Oxford I wilted at the sight of a pub lout, while here I can face a horde of the enemy and strike them down.*

He turned back to the German trench.

*No striking them down today.*

He spread out his hands, palms toward the Germans, and took a few steps forward.

*"Sehr gut, kamarade!"* one of them shouted.

He and a couple of others clambered out of the trench and paused, looking back at their trench and probably thinking the same things he had. Like Thompson, whoever the commander was over there was either too surprised or too impressed to object.

"Oi, where you think you're going?"

Crawford was out of the trench and hurrying up to him.

"Bit more roomy up here, innit?" he said as he came up. His face was pale, eyes wide, and there was a broad, nervous smile across his face.

"Glad to see you didn't bring your gun," Willoughby said.

"What, you think I'm an idiot?"

"Don't make me answer that. Let's go meet them halfway, shall we?"

They started walking slowly across No Man's Land, a place where men only crawl or run. The ground was pitted with shell craters and strewn with the trash of two armies. Rusting weapons and discarded bits of kit lay everywhere. The low humps of the dead were mingled with the debris. The ground was rough and frozen. They had to watch their step.

"This is mad," Crawford said, shaking his head in wonder.

"No madder than everything else we've been through in the past four months."

Several Germans were walking towards them. They, too, had left their rifles behind. Willoughby glanced over his shoulder and saw a few more English soldiers climbing out of the trench.

"You don't have that Moroccan knife under your greatcoat, do you?" Crawford asked in a low voice.

"Oh, bloody hell!"

"Just don't flash it around. They might get tetchy."

Willoughby gulped. No, he wouldn't flash it around, or this whole thing would end badly. He was amazed it hadn't already.

A couple of the Germans came up to them, waving and smiling.

"Merry Christmas, Tommy!" one said in German.

"Merry Christmas to you too," Willoughby replied.

The fellow had an amazed, slightly stunned look to his face, like he couldn't believe what he was doing. Willoughby felt the same.

For a moment everyone fell into silent smiles and shy looks. One of the Germans extended his hand and said in English, "My name is Hans."

"Pleased to meet you, Hans," Willoughby said, shaking it.

Crawford grinned and pointed to a small barrel a little larger than a football hanging from a strap around Hans' shoulder.

"Oi, is that what I think it is?"

"You must be Crawford," the man said with a grin. "Yes, this is some good German beer from my hometown of Stuttgart."

"Then I'm pleased to meet you, Hans," Crawford took his hand and pumped it. "Hey, Willoughby, you got the bottle?"

Willoughby was already pulling it out of the pocket of his greatcoat. Just as he did so, he realized that he had made what could have been construed as a hostile move. The two Germans had watched his hand, but didn't seem unduly alarmed.

*This is actually happening,* his sense of wonder growing every minute.

He held up the bottle of Scotch.

"Drink?" he asked.

"Don't mind if we do."

A few more British and Germans started gathering. About a hundred yards away, another group was gathering.

"Did anyone bring their cups?" Willoughby asked.

Blank faces all around. Hans repeated the question in German and got a similar response. Willoughby shrugged.

"Fuck it."

Willoughby popped off the cork and took a slug. The Scotch bit at his throat, then spread a warmth through his insides.

He offered it to Hans, who took a slug and gave it to Crawford. As the bottle went around, the little barrel of beer starting going around too.

*I've never been drunk before noon. I suppose this is as good a time as any.*

Already the alcohol was giving him a pleasant haze. Everyone was chatting in two languages regardless of whether they understood it or not. Crawford and Hans were laughing about some joke he didn't catch. A few others were trading cigarettes. The other group a hundred yards away had linked arms and were singing carols.

Through the crowd of smiling faces he saw another group of Germans clamber out of their trench. One was an older man with a large handlebar moustache and the strict military air of a career soldier, as well as the proud bearing of an aristocrat. Next to him was a huge fellow, who from the soles of his boots to the tip of his *Pickelhaube* must have been at least seven feet. Following them came four more men. All had the steely, determined eyes and the easy, precise movements of veterans. Even from a distance Willoughby could see they wore no insignia, not even the man who was so obviously their officer.

Crawford was staring too.

"Is that them?" Willoughby asked.

Crawford nodded and took a step forward.

A hand grasped his shoulder. Major Thompson.

"Steady," Thompson said, and strode towards the German raiding team. Willoughby and Crawford fell in behind him. Within a few steps Black and Fisher caught up. The Germans came right for them, each man sizing up the others. No weapons were visible. Willoughby wasn't fooled.

"Spirit of the season, gentlemen," Thompson said under his breath.

As they came within ten yards of each other, both teams stopped as if by some unspoken accord. Thompson and the German officer met in the middle. Just beyond them lay a dead body. Covered as it was by mud and frost, it was impossible to tell the color of the uniform. It lay curled in one itself, facing neither trench.

"Hello," Thompson said. "I'm afraid my German is a bit rusty."

"Hello, it is no matter," the German replied in precise, heavily accented English. "I studied for a time in London."

Both men paused. The German came to attention and saluted. Thompson returned the salute half a second later. They shook hands. They took their time letting go.

With a slow, clear movement, Thompson reached into his breast pocket and pulled out a packet of cigarettes.

"Smoke?"

"Ah, Woodbines! I have missed them. I always smoked them in London."

"Take the packet then." Thompson handed it to him.

"That is most kind."

Both men were still stiff as if at attention, sizing each other up and not taking their eyes off one another. The German officer reached into his pocket and brought out a gold cigarette case. He emptied it of its contents and offered them to Thompson.

"A very nice brand called Sultan's Delight, from our Ottoman allies."

"Most kind of you."

Crawford muttered under his breath to Willoughby. "Bit awkward, innit? They're like a pair of marionettes."

Willoughby wasn't sure if it was the alcohol, the holiday, or the foolish urge he had felt ever since the doctor had asked him if he were fit for service. Perhaps it was all three, but he found himself striding forward with the bottle in his hand.

The two officers turned to him. He snapped out a salute.

"Would you and your men like some Scotch?" he asked in German.

The officer gave a little smile, turned and called out the question in German to his team. The big brute who seemed to be his second in command roared out his approval and waved a bottle of schnapps over his head.

"That's more like it!" Crawford called out.

Within moments the two groups had mingled. Suddenly everyone was exchanging cigarettes. A couple more bottles magically appeared.

The mood, however, was not the same as it was with the first gathering. These were not anonymous members of the opposing army, distant figures now turned into friendly faces. They had met in close combat, and both sides had lost comrades. That they would meet again, no one was in any doubt.

Willoughby found himself translating for his friends. He noticed one German fellow, smaller than the rest and with an air of education about him, spoke only in German but appeared to be listening attentively when people spoke in English.

Crawford had paired up with the giant German, his five-and-a-half foot frame looking like a child's next to the seven-foot brute. Neither spoke the other's language but they were getting along just fine with the universal language of tobacco and alcohol.

Smoke hung everywhere. He found the Germans' cigarettes, with their Turkish tobacco, made him cough even more than regular cigarettes.

*Bloody hell,* he thought, waving his hand in front of his face. *It's like they're trying to kill us with poison fumes.*

Lunch came. Neither side seemed inclined to go back to their trenches so the food was brought to the men brave enough to meet in the middle. Willoughby got to have sausage and sauerkraut while the Germans ate some of their bully beef.

Theirs wasn't the only group sitting together. Looking to either side, he could see several other groups spread out along the line. Most men stayed in their own trenches, however, although the pluckier ones sat on the parapet. The more practical busied themselves clearing bodies from No Man's Land. He saw Captain Dickson commanding one burial party, doing his share of carrying the dead. Willoughby's estimation of him rose a little.

Once lunch was finished, someone in the group next to them produced a football. Soon a dozen Englishmen and Germans were kicking it around, laughing and slipping on the frosty ground.

The little German who pretended he didn't speak English leapt up.

"Let's play a proper match!" he urged his comrades in German.

He gave a significant look to a sly-looking fellow Black had been keeping an eye on. The fellow nodded and they gathered up a few more people. Black grabbed Crawford.

"It's the Kings versus the Kaisers, lad. I hope you kick better than you drive."

"I'd kick you right in the arse if you weren't on my side."

Willoughby hoped no one called on him to play. He was having too good a time to make a fool of himself.

Both teams started to gather, made up mostly of the two raiding parties. Greatcoats were used to mark out two goals, the English goal near their own trench and the German goal near theirs.

Willoughby smiled when he noticed that No Man's Land was only slightly longer than a football pitch.

Then he noticed something else. If the English got a goal, they'd get a good look at the German trench, and vice versa.

Nothing had been said, but the sharper minds on either side had set this up.

Major Thompson and the German officer stormed forward.

*"Nein! Nein!"*

"None of this, gentlemen," Thompson said.

"It's just a kickabout, sir," Black protested.

"It's unsportsmanlike," Thompson said.

"Unsportsmanlike? I haven't even committed a foul yet," Black muttered.

The German officer spoke to his own men.

"We're not going to sour this Christmas with this sort of thing."

The giant German laughed. "But they want to, sir!"

"I forbid it, and so does their officer. We'll see their trench soon enough."

The men shrugged and the game broke up. Soon everyone was back to drinking and smoking. From the distance, carols in both languages floated over the cratered ground.

It was getting late and it would be dark soon. Willoughby realized they had spent most of the short winter's day together in No Man's Land. Soon it would be time to go back to their respective trenches.

Willoughby turned to the small, intelligent looking man. The fellow studied him, a slight smile tugging at his lips.

"Nice try with joining that football match," Willoughby said in English. "Too bad our commanders called it off."

*"Nicht verstehen,"* The German replied, putting on a poor imitation of a confused expression.

"Yes, you understand. I suspect you wouldn't have been able to get through our defense in any case. I was never very good at games myself. Good at lessons, though, and my tutors told me I have a natural ear for languages. Did they say the same to you?"

*"Nicht verstehen."*

Willoughby's voice grew softer. "It's strange. I never thought I'd be good at this. Just look at me. But I've led several raids on you chaps and they've all succeeded, more or less."

The German didn't reply. He was meeting Willoughby's eye now.

"Perhaps it's the same with you. In fact, you remind me of a chap in our Anglo-German Society at Oxford. He was a foreign student from East Prussia. Bright fellow. Always sat in the same section of the Bodleian Library as I did. I suspect he's somewhere on the line with you chaps now. I could tell you his name but perhaps I shouldn't. The thing is, it could have been you sitting in the Bodleian or chatting about history at our weekly meetings over drinks at the Eagle and Child. Pity we're not there now."

The German reached into his breast pocket and pulled out a small brass object. Willoughby blinked when he saw it was a tie pin. Even more, it was a King's College tie pin.

*Oh Lord, a Cambridge man. That makes it easier, I suppose.*

The German presented it to him. Willoughby took it and paused. What could he give him back? He rummaged around his pockets and could only find his pocketbook. Opening it up, he spotted a postcard his sister had sent him showing Magdalen College.

"Here. Compliments of that other university."

The German grinned.

Major Thompson's voice rang out. "We should get going."

Willoughby noticed it was getting dark. The German officer started collecting his men.

"Well," Willoughby said to the German who had studied at Cambridge. "I suppose this is good-bye. Or at least, 'until next time'. I don't suppose I'll get a good-bye in English, will I?"

The German smiled again. Looking over his shoulder, he saw his comrades heading back to the trench, the officer well out of earshot. He turned back to Willoughby, extended his hand, and in clear English without a trace of an accent said two words.

"No hatred."

Willoughby shook his hand.

"Never," he replied.

*From a Christmas feast, a warm hearth, and gifts to. . .this.*

*I'm where I belong.*

The German turned and followed his comrades back to their trench.

"Oi, Willoughby!" Crawford called. "You going to stand out here all night?"

"I'm coming."

He, too, was the last of his side to leave. As he strolled back to the trench, he knew why he hadn't asked to stay in England. Not for this, of course, he could have never predicted this. No, he had come back to spend Christmas with Company E. And it had served a purpose. They had met the other raiding party and he had learned a little bit about them. Like what their men were like, and the fact that they hadn't glanced at the observation trench the entire time, showing they knew all about it. And the fact that one of them could speak English without an accent, like he could speak German like a native. That sort of knowledge about the other raiding party would be useful.

He knew that if he survived the war this Christmas Day ceasefire would turn into the stuff of legend. That abortive football match would take on epic proportions. The numbers of men coming out of the trench would grow from companies to entire battalions. And few would remember the sly looks and attempts to get closer to each other's trenches. The war had paused for breath, but had never left their minds.

Wouldn't it be grand, though, if this lasted? If a Christmas in No Man's Land would stop the war?

But he knew it wouldn't. There probably wouldn't be any firing tomorrow, and little the next day. But the day after that? No, it wouldn't last to the day after that. It would be back to the war then.

Back to what he was good at.

At least he would have his friends with him. At least he could help them get through another day. Back home he was loved, but not needed. Here it was different.

Night was gathering quickly now. He reached the parapet of the trench and sat down on it. He looked over his shoulder at the German trench and waved.

"Come on, Willoughby," Black said. He sat not far off, his face illuminated by the soft glow of Fisher's spirit stove. All his friends were gathered around it. "Stop consorting with the enemy and have a cup of tea. We have some schnapps for it."

Willoughby jumped down into the trench and joined his friends.


Follow more adventures of Company E in the Trench Raiders series: *Trench Raiders*, *Digging In*, and *No Man's Land*.

## AUTHOR'S NOTE

The Christmas Truce of 1914 was a key moment in World War One. After four months of unparalleled savagery and losses, men on both sides took a day off to remember what peacetime was like. History books and documentaries tend to exaggerate the extent of the truce, however. While many parts of the line went quiet that day, fighting continued elsewhere. Only in a few special spots did the men get out of their trenches and fraternize. The high commands of both sides saw this as a threat to discipline and in 1915 issued strict orders for it not to happen again. Christmas 1915 saw no Christmas Truce.

While the Oxfordshire and Buckinghamshire Light Infantry was a real unit whose 2$^{nd}$ battalion fought at Ypres, E Company and all its members are fictitious. In fact, battalions only had four companies, but E Company is exceptional in many ways! All other units and major operations depicted in this story are real, as are many smaller details. I've taken one major artistic liberty—the regiment was actually in billets behind the line during Christmas 1914. Of course, after all Willoughby and his pals have been through, I couldn't resist the temptation to have them witness one of the most extraordinary events of the war. I hope the fictional heroics of Major Thompson and his men in some small way reflect the real-life valor of the men of the "Ox and Bucks".

My principal sources for this story have been Alan Wakefield's *Christmas in the Trenches* and Simon Harris' excellent *History of the 43$^{rd}$ and 52$^{nd}$ (Oxfordshire and Buckinghamshire) Light Infantry in the Great War, Volume II: Operations in France and Belgium*. I beg the indulgence of these specialists for any artistic liberties I have taken with their areas of research.

# Want to read some of my books for free?

If you sign up for my newsletter[1], *Sean's Travels and Tales*, you get TWO FREE EBOOKS—the historical mystery *Tangier Bank Heist* and the post-apocalyptic science fiction *Radio Hope*. In addition, each monthly issue features a short story or travel article, a coupon for a free or discounted book, and updates on future projects. How cool is that? You can subscribe using this link[2]. Your email will not be shared with anyone else.

---

1. https://books.bookfunnel.com/seanmclachlan
2. https://books.bookfunnel.com/seanmclachlan

# About the Author

Sean McLachlan worked for ten years as an archaeologist in Israel, Cyprus, Bulgaria, and the United States before becoming a full-time writer. He is the author of numerous fiction and nonfiction books, which are listed on the following pages. When he's not writing, he enjoys hiking, reading, traveling, and, most of all, teaching his son about the world. He divides his time between Madrid, Oxford, and Cairo.

To find out more about Sean's work and travels, visit him at his website[1], Amazon page[2], or blog[3], and feel free to friend him on Goodreads[4] and Facebook[5]. And don't forget to nab two free ebooks by subscribing to his newsletter[6]! Your email won't be shared with anyone.

---

1. https://www.seanmclachlan.net/
2. http://www.amazon.com/Sean-McLachlan/e/B001H6MUQI/
3. http://midlistwriter.blogspot.com
4. http://www.goodreads.com/author/show/623273.Sean_McLachlan
5. https://www.facebook.com/writersean
6. https://books.bookfunnel.com/seanmclachlan

# Fiction by Sean McLachlan

*Trench Raiders (Trench Raiders Book One)*

September 1914: The British Expeditionary Force has the Germans on the run, or so they think.

After a month of bitter fighting, the British are battered, exhausted, and down to half their strength, yet they've helped save Paris and are pushing towards Berlin. Then the retreating Germans decide to make a stand. Holding a steep slope beside the River Aisne, the entrenched Germans mow down the advancing British with machine gun fire. Soon the British dig in too, and it looks like the war might grind down into deadly stalemate.

Searching through No-Man's Land in the darkness, Private Timothy Crawford of the Oxfordshire and Buckinghamshire Light Infantry finds a chink in the German armor. But can this lowly private, who spends as much time in the battalion guardhouse as he does on the parade ground, convince his commanding officer to risk everything for a chance to break through?

*Available in electronic and print editions!*


*Digging In (Trench Raiders Book Two)*

October 1914: The British line is about to break.

After two months of hard fighting, the British Expeditionary Force is short of men, ammunition, and ideas. With their line stretched to the breaking point, aerial reconnaissance spots German reinforcements massing for the big push. As their trenches are hammered by a German artillery battery, the men of the Oxfordshire and Buckinghamshire Light Infantry come up with a desperate plan—a daring raid behind enemy lines to destroy the enemy guns and give the British a chance to stop the German army from breaking through.

*Available in electronic and print editions!*


*No Man's Land (Trench Raiders Book Three)*

No Man's Land—a hellscape of shell craters and dead bodies. Soldiers have fought over it, charged across it, and bled on it for a year of grueling war, but neither side has dominated it.

Until now.

An elite German raiding party is passing through No Man's Land every night, attacking the British trenches at will. The Oxfordshire and Buckinghamshire Light Infantry need to reassert control over their front lines.

So the exhausted men of Company E decide to set a trap, a nighttime ambush in the middle of No Man's Land, where any mistake can be fatal. But the few surviving veterans are leading recruits who have only been in the trenches for two weeks. Mistakes are inevitable.

*Available in electronic and print editions!*


*Christmas Truce*

Christmas 1914

In the cold, muddy trenches of the Western Front, there is a strange silence. As the members of a crack English trench raiding team enjoy their first day of peace in months, they call out holiday greetings to the men on the German line. Soon both sides are fraternizing in No Man's Land.

But when the English recognize some enemy raiders who only a few days before launched a deadly attack on their position, can they keep the peace through the Christmas truce?

*Available in electronic and print editions!*

*Warpath into Sonora*

Arizona 1846

Nantan, a young Apache warrior, is building a name for himself by leading raids against Mexican ranches to impress his war chief, and the chief's lovely daughter. But there is one thing he and all other Apaches fear—a ruthless band of Mexican scalp hunters who slaughter entire villages.

Nantan and his friends have sworn to fight back, but they are inexperienced, and led by a war chief driven mad with a thirst for revenge. Can they track their tribe's worst enemy into unknown territory and defeat them?

*Available in electronic and print editions!*

*The Case of the Purloined Pyramid (The Masked Man of Cairo Book One)*

An ancient mystery. A modern murder.

Sir Augustus Wall, a horribly mutilated veteran of the Great War, has left Europe behind to open an antiquities shop in Cairo. But Europe's troubles follow him as a priceless inscription is stolen and those who know its secrets start turning up dead. Teaming up with Egyptology expert Moustafa Ghani, and Faisal, an irritating street urchin he just can't shake, Sir Wall must unravel an ancient secret and face his own dark past.

*Available in electronic and print editions!*

*The Case of the Shifting Sarcophagus (The Masked Man of Cairo Book Two)*

An Old Kingdom coffin. A body from yesterday.

Sir Augustus Wall had seen a lot of death. From the fields of Flanders to the alleys of Cairo, he'd solved several murders and sent many men to their grave. But he's never had a body delivered to his antiquities shop encased in a 5,000 year-old coffin.

Soon he finds himself fighting a vicious street gang bent on causing national mayhem while his assistant, Moustafa Ghani, faces his own enemies in the form of colonial powers determined to ruin him. Throughout all this runs the street urchin Faisal. Ignored as usual, dismissed as usual, he has the most important fight of all.

*Available in electronic and print editions!*


*The Case of the Golden Greeks (The Masked Man of Cairo Book Three)*

They thought the case was solved.

When an eminent Egyptologist is murdered giving a lecture in front of a packed hall, Cairo's chief of police quickly rounds up those responsible.

Or at least some of them.

Sir Augustus Wall, antiquities dealer and amateur sleuth, knows there's more to the crime than it seems. With little to go on but an exotic murder weapon, a map of a desert oasis, and some gilded Greek mummies, he sets out across the Sahara with his assistant Moustafa Ghani and the street urchin Faisal, who is the only person to have seen the killer's face. They soon find themselves in the midst of international intrigue on Egypt's remote border with Libya.

Can they discover what mystery lies beneath Bahariya Oasis?

*Available in electronic and print editions!*


*The Case of the Karnak Killer (The Masked Man of Cairo Book Four)*

A scandal in America. A murder in Cairo.

Sir Augustus Wall, antiquities dealer and amateur sleuth, is hired to track down a blackmailer who threatens the reputation of an American millionaire. When blackmail turns to murder, he must travel up the Nile by steamboat to find the killer.

Joining him are Faisal, a street urchin who makes himself equally useful and troublesome; Heinrich Schäfer, a leading Egyptologist; and Jocelyn Montjoy, an adventurous woman who has captured his heart.

But complications set in before the hunt even begins. Unwelcome fellow passengers threaten to derail the investigation, and Augustus has fallen out with his right-hand man, Moustafa Ghani. Can a new team of investigators help him solve his most challenging case yet?

*Available in electronic and print editions!*

*The Case of the Asphyxiated Alexandrian (The Masked Man of Cairo Book 5)*

A mysterious murder. A lost pharaoh.

Sir Augustus Wall came to Egypt to escape his old life, but when a comrade from the trenches is found murdered in a Cairo hotel, Augustus realizes his past has finally caught up.

Now he must discover the reason for the baffling murder, leading him and his friends Moustafa and Faisal on a dangerous hunt for the most sought-after treasure in Egypt.

The long-awaited fifth book in the Masked Man of Cairo series sees the trio on their greatest adventure yet!

*Available in electronic and print editions!*

*The Case of the Dastardly Djinn (A Masked Man of Cairo Prequel)*

A homeless boy. A hunted girl.

Cairo, 1917. In a city plagued by poverty and war, ten-year-old Faisal begs and steals to survive, hiding at night from the things that prowl after dark. The nimblest and most clever of the street boys, he's terrified of the unseen spirits he's convinced haunt the ancient city.

But when he discovers a girl his age left homeless by a terrible tragedy, Faisal decides to do what no one ever did for him—help. With no shelter and facing the many dangers of Cairo's darkened streets, Faisal's loyalties are tested when together they uncover a criminal ring more sinister than his worst superstitions.

This prequel to the Masked Man of Cairo mystery adventure series will thrill new readers and long-time fans alike!

A portion of the proceeds from this book will go to help Egyptian street children.

*Available in electronic and print editions!*


*Tangier Bank Heist: An Interzone Mystery*

Right after the war, Tangier was the craziest town in North Africa. Everything was for sale and the price was cheap. The perverts came for the flesh. The addicts came for the drugs. A whole army of hustlers and grifters came for the loose laws and free flow of cash and contraband.

So why was I here? Because it was the only place that would have me. Besides, it was a great place to be a detective. You got cases like in no other place I'd ever been, and I'd been all over. Cases you couldn't believe ever happened. Like when I had to track down the guy who stole the bank.

No, he didn't rob the bank, he stole it.

Here's how it happened . . .

*Available in electronic and print editions!*


*Three Passports to Trouble (Interzone Mystery Book 2)*

Back in the days when Tangier was an International Zone, the city was full of refugees. People fleeing Stalin. People fleeing Franco. People fleeing the Nuremburg Trials. Tangier offered a safe haven from the chaos of Europe.

The International Council had to keep a delicate balance, tolerating everything from anti-capitalist agitators to Germans with murky pasts. It was the only way to keep the peace, and it worked.

Until an anarchist was found dead with a fascist dagger in his chest.

And I got stuck with the case just when I had to smuggle a couple of Party operatives out of town.

*Available in electronic and print editions!*


*Flight to Fez (Interzone Mystery Book Three)*

Only in Tangier could a literary event turn into a murder scene.

I'm "Shorty" MacAllister, private detective. I've investigated all sorts of crazy cases in this lawless town, tracking down con men and Nazi fugitives, anarchists and bank robbers, all the while running my own secret angle.

But I never thought that when I went to hear my friend Jane Bowles read her latest story I'd end with a murdered man in my lap, and an old war buddy getting pinned with the crime.

After that, things got a whole lot more complicated.

*Available in electronic and print editions!*


*A Winter Murder in Berlin (The Berlin Murders Book One)*

The voyage of a lifetime turns into a nightmare.

When Katherine Schmidt sails for Europe in late 1929, she looks forward to a year of carefree travel thanks to an unexpected inheritance. But when a companion on her steamer is murdered and she becomes a suspect, she needs to find the real killer before the police close in. Now she must delve into Weimar Berlin's decadent nightlife and radical politics in order to clear her name.

Can an innocent young woman from Missouri outwit fascists, communists, and the denizens of Berlin's notorious shadow world?

*Available in electronic and print editions!*


*Radio Hope (Toxic World Book One)*
In a world shattered by war, pollution and disease...

A gunslinging mother longs to find a safe refuge for her son.

A frustrated revolutionary delivers water to villagers living on a toxic waste dump.

The assistant mayor of humanity's last city hopes he will never have to take command.

One thing gives them the promise of a better future—Radio Hope, a mysterious station that broadcasts vital information about surviving in a blighted world. But when a mad prophet and his army of fanatics march out of the wildlands on a crusade to purify the land with blood and fire, all three will find their lives intertwining, and changing forever.

*Available in print and electronic editions!*


*Refugees from the Righteous Horde (Toxic World Book Two)*
When you only have one shot, you better aim true.

In a ravaged world, civilization's last outpost is reeling after fighting off the fanatical warriors of the Righteous Horde. Sheriff Annette Cruz becomes New City's long arm of vengeance as she sets off across the wildlands to take out the cult's leader. All she has is a sniper's rifle with one bullet and a former cultist with his own agenda. Meanwhile, one of the cult's escaped slaves makes a discovery that could tear New City apart...

*Available in electronic and print editions!*


*We Had Flags (Toxic World Book Three)*
A law doesn't work if everyone breaks it.

For forty years, New City has been a bastion of order in a fallen world. One crucial law has maintained the peace: it is illegal to place responsibility for the collapse of civilization on any one group. Anyone found guilty of Blaming is branded and stripped of citizenship.

But when some unwelcome visitors arrive from across the sea, old wounds break open, and no one is safe from Blame.

*Available in electronic and print editions!*

*Emergency Transmission (Toxic World Book Four)*

Trust is the only thing that can save the world.

The problem is, everyone has their own agenda.

When an offshore platform starts emitting toxic fumes that threaten to destroy the last outposts of civilization, the residents of New City have to team up with a foreign freighter to fix it. But a lingering mistrust remains, and neither side has the resources to stop the leak.

That is, until help comes from the least reliable source.

Can old enemies finally set aside their differences for the greater good?

*Available in electronic and print editions!*

*Tales from the Toxic World*

A scavenger with a wondrous artifact from the Old Times sets out to avenge his past ...

The sheriff of a post-apocalyptic shantytown investigates a baffling murder ...

Two fishermen in a toxic sea make a startling discovery ...

A peddler has to compromise his faith to help others and not end up dead ...

Here are nine stories from a grim future that's all too possible. The world has been destroyed by war, pollution, and environmental degradation. Now only a few lonely outposts struggle to keep the light of civilization lit amid vast toxic wasteland filled with human predators.

This collection is a long-awaited addition to the popular Toxic World post-apocalyptic science fiction series. It's sure to please fans and newcomers to the series alike.

*Available in electronic and print editions!*


*The Scavenger (A Toxic World Novelette)*

In a world shattered by war, pollution, and disease, a lone scavenger discovers a priceless relic from the Old Times.

The problem is, it's stuck in the middle of the worst wasteland he knows—a contaminated city inhabited by insane chem addicts and vengeful villagers. Only his wits, his gun, and an unlikely ally can get him out alive.

Set in the Toxic World series introduced in the novel *Radio Hope*, this 10,000-word story explores more of the dangers and personalities that make up a post-apocalyptic world that's all too possible.

*Available in electronic and print editions!*


*A Fine Likeness (House Divided Book One)*

A Confederate guerrilla and a Union captain discover there's something more dangerous in the woods than each other.

Jimmy Rawlins is a teenage bushwhacker who leads his friends on ambushes of Union patrols. They join infamous guerrilla leader Bloody Bill Anderson on a raid through Missouri, but Jimmy questions his commitment to the cause when he discovers this madman plans to sacrifice a Union prisoner in a hellish ritual to raise the Confederate dead.

Richard Addison is an aging captain of a lackluster Union militia. Depressed over his son's death in battle, a glimpse of Jimmy changes his life. Jimmy and his son look so much alike that Addison becomes obsessed with saving him from Bloody Bill. Captain Addison must wreck his reputation to win this war within a war, while Jimmy must decide whether to betray the Confederacy to stop the evil arising in the woods of Missouri.

*Available in print and electronic editions!*


*The River of Desperation (House Divided Book Two)*

In the waning days of the Civil War, a secret conflict still rages...

Lieutenant Allen Addison of the *USS Essex* is looking forward to the South's defeat so he can build the life he's always wanted. Love and a promising business await him in St. Louis, but he is swept up in a primeval war between the forces of Order and Chaos, a struggle he doesn't understand and can barely believe in. Soon he is fighting to keep a grip on his sanity as he tries to save St. Louis from destruction.

The long-awaited sequel to *A Fine Likeness* continues the story of two opposing forces that threaten to tear the world apart.

*Available in electronic and print editions!*


*The Last Hotel Room*

He came to Tangier to die, but life isn't done with him yet.

Tom Miller has lost his job, his wife, and his dreams. Broke and alone, he ends up in a flophouse in Morocco, ready to end it all. But soon he finds himself tangled in a web of danger and duty as he's pulled into scamming tourists for a crooked cop while trying to help a Syrian refugee boy survive life on the streets. Can a lifelong loser do something good for a change?

A portion of my royalties will go to a charity for Syrian refugees.

*Available in electronic and print editions!*

*The Night the Nazis Came to Dinner and Other Dark Tales*

A spectral dinner party goes horribly wrong...

An immortal warrior hopes a final battle will set him free...

A big-game hunter preys on endangered species to supply an illicit restaurant...

A new technology soothes First World guilt...

Here are four dark tales that straddle the boundary between reality and speculation. You better hope they don't come true.

*Available in electronic edition!*


*The Quintessence of Absence*

Can a drug-addicted sorcerer sober up long enough to save a kidnapped girl and his own duchy?

In an alternate eighteenth-century Germany where magic is real and paganism never died, Lothar is in the bonds of nepenthe, a powerful drug that gives him ecstatic visions. It has also taken his job, his friends, and his self-respect. Now his old employer has rehired Lothar to find the man's daughter, who is in the grip of her own addiction to nepenthe.

As Lothar digs deeper into the girl's disappearance, he uncovers a plot that threatens the entire Duchy of Anhalt, and finds that the only way to stop it is to face his own weakness.

*Available in electronic edition!*

# Writing Books by Sean McLachlan

*Writing Secrets of the World's Most Prolific Authors*

What does it take to write 100 books? What about 500? Or 1,000?

That may sound like an impossibly high number, but it isn't. Some of the world's most successful authors wrote hundreds of books over the course of highly lucrative careers. Isaac Asimov wrote more than 300 books. Enid Blyton wrote more than 800. Legendary Western writer Lauren Bosworth Paine wrote close to 1,000.

Some wrote even more.

This book examines the techniques and daily habits of more than a dozen of these remarkable writers to show how anyone with the right mindset can massively increase their word count without sacrificing quality. Learn the secrets of working on several projects simultaneously, of reducing the time needed for each book, and how to build the work ethic you need to become more prolific than you ever thought possible.

*Available in electronic and print edition!*

# History Books by Sean McLachlan

Wild West History
*Apache Warrior vs. US Cavalryman: 1846-86* (Osprey: 2016)
*Tombstone—Wyatt Earp, the O.K. Corral, and the Vendetta Ride*
(Osprey: 2013)
*The Last Ride of the James-Younger Gang* (Osprey: 2012)
Civil War History
*Ride Around Missouri: Shelby's Great Raid 1863* (Osprey: 2011)
*American Civil War Guerrilla Tactics* (Osprey: 2009)
Missouri History
*Outlaw Tales of Missouri* (Globe Pequot: 2009)
*Missouri: An Illustrated History* (Hippocrene: 2008)
*It Happened in Missouri* (Globe Pequot: 2007)
Medieval History
*Medieval Handgonnes: The First Black Powder Infantry Weapons*
(Osprey: 2010)
*Byzantium: An Illustrated History* (Hippocrene: 2004)
African History
*Armies of the Adowa Campaign 1896: The Italian Disaster in Ethiopia*
(Osprey: 2011)